Window To New Birth

50th Century's Prodigies

A NOBLE CAPTAIN BOURN
EPISODE (4)

By

Sarah Teresa Vaughan

About the Author

Sarah Teresa Vaughan is a young writer. She has 22q11.2 Micro Deletion Syndrome, also known as Di George Syndrome, Asperger's, and Sensory Integration Dysfunction, which she believes give her a unique perspective of the world. She was born in Shakopee, MN. She nearly died as an infant, and continues to suffer illnesses.

She lives with her Mother, Paulette, in Bemidji, whom homeschooled her. She graduated at the Prior Lake Baptist Church in Prior Lake, MN, in 2002. She has been writing as young as five. She was a little girl with a huge imagination, even before she wrote. She continues to be a prolific reader, and an obsessed writer. As young as ten, she fell in love with William Shakespeare, his works creating in her, the desire to learn Elizabethan English. She read his original works such as *A Mid Summer-Night's Dream*, and *King Lear* for the mere fun. By the time she reached her mid twenties, she read half of his plays, and all of his sonnets. Poetry has always been her love. Since her early school days, she has immensely enjoyed dictionaries and lexicons. Since 2003, she has attended classes at the Head Waters School Of Music And Arts in Bemidji. Her first book, *Where Is Reality? An Aspie Poet Asks*, is a collection of her early poems, in a variety of forms. One of her goals with her writing is to reintroduce the Elizabethan language back into the literary world. Colouring and drawing are a few other pastimes.

A love for Elvis Presley, and his songs, grew her love for music into an avid scale. She enjoys playing the balalaika, Spanish classical guitar, piano, and violin. *Mikrokosmos* by Béla Bartók is a favorite series of books she enjoys in piano.

At thirty years old, she began receiving Neuro-Optometric Therapy. For this therapy, she wears lenses of yoked base down prism/ midline shift. This found blessing, saved her eyesight. The lenses enable her to see depth, dimension, and texture. Now, living in two different worlds, her art work, and hobbies have expanded.

She is self taught in philosophy, and learning to read and write in several foreign languages, for the mere fun. Through workbooks, at home, she learns: French, Greek, Italian, Biblical Latin, Classical Latin, Latin American, Mexican, and Spanish International, her current forté.

Science fiction is also a passion of hers. This is her first book of science fiction she has out, *50th Century's Prodigies A Noble Captain Bourn Episode 4*. She believes these are gifts from God.

Intro

When I was first approached by Carol Ann Russell to provide this Introduction to Sarah's book, **50th Century's Prodigies A Noble Captain Bourn (Episode 4)**, I knew I was in for a treat. I had heard about Sarah's talents and struggle, prior and now had the chance to find out and comment upon it all first hand. I mean, here's what my former Bemidji State University English instructor Mark Christianson had to say about **Where Is Reality?** on Amazon:

> "I jumped in my chair, startled by a poem handed to me in a one-day writing workshop I was teaching. The view of reality in that poem was unlike any I had encountered. A few years later I read a book of poems by that young woman, Sarah Vaughan, and am startled once again. These are strange poems, poems of faith found in action figures, women waving scarves, phantoms of the living dead. Read them, and discover reality as you have never known it."
> _**Where Is Reality? An Aspie Poet Asks**

And Mark doesn't jump from his chair often, believe me. Now for those of you who may be unaware of what *I* do and if I am qualified to handle this assignment, here is currently what I have on my Amazon Author Page:

Roy C. Booth hails from Bemidji, MN where he manages Roy's Comics & Games (est. 1992) with his wife and three sons. He is a published author, comedian, poet, journalist, essayist, screenwriter, and internationally awarded playwright with nearly 60 plays published (Samuel French Heuer, et al) with 800+ productions worldwide in 29 countries in ten languages. He is also known for collaborations with R Thomas Riley, Brian Keene, Eric M. Heideman, William F. Wu, Axel Kohagen, and others (along with his presence on the regional convention circuit). See his entry on Wikipedia, his Facebook page, and his publisher's sites for more.

And there we go.

The book you have in your hands is a unique hybrid of poetry, prose, and Plautine playwrighting set in a fantastic science fiction setting that has been painstakingly researched and lovingly constructed. This edition marks a golden opportunity for a far wider audience to enjoy Sarah's writings in a format well suited for the commute, the fireplace, or even the bedsheets.

What makes this project even more unique is that Sarah has infused it with a variety of poetic and literary forms from sonnets to odes to even the dirge, some of them not quite familiar with modern readers, but well known to poets. For example, she makes use of the rather complex sestina…

> **…a poem with six stanzas of six lines and a final triplet, all stanzas having the same six words at the line-ends in six different sequences that follow a fixed pattern, and with all six words appearing in the closing three-line envoi.**

Pretty stylized and precise writing, to be sure.

Sarah also experiments with lesser known forms, such as the English roundelay, which is traditionally a 24 line poem that makes use of refrains and two rhyme sounds in trochaic tetrameter. In this case, she incorporates its fundamental principles into crisp, moving dialog. And here is an actual sample of Sarah's blend of poetry and prose for a desired narrative effect:

The Spectacle Of An Infant Prodigy Of Space
Narrative Poem

There is a spectacle here, at the Purple Awards Center. Her name is Alika, and she is one year old. Yesternight, she saved lives aboard the star ship, *Velocity*. This most popular ship is one of the main targets of Planet Gauss. She was visiting as a guest. It was a celebration for Alika. Having gifts for her and cheering the fortunate 101-year old brother, neither he nor the crew knew the fierce Gaussian war vessel was going to kill them. After Alika baffles all with a mature greeting, mentioning the word "honour," she points out the two-dimensional monstrous ship that would have destroyed all.

At the Purple Awards Center, Alika is the first infant in history to receive a crown, which wilt not fit until she is much older, for her service to Planet Tar and Tar's moons. Asking Captain V fan how they might be greeted at home, he answers, "Alika will get all attention, and I might be in BIG trouble with Mom, and Dad."
      Iwis, Forbearance Missive Report

Now, even here, we have a good sense of Postmodern whimsy, from an unlikely (and improbable!) infant protagonist to a profound difference in sibling ages to a seasoned star ship captain musing upon his possible treatment upon completing the voyage home. Each snippet within the snippet alludes to a unique story unto its own, rife with "what if…?" double takes and myriad possibilities.

To take this unusual, daring excerpt even further, I shared it, along with other scenes, with some of my writing industry friends, and colleagues at this years' MarsCon, held March 4-6 at the Hilton Minneapolis/St. Paul Airport/Mall Of America. Seeing as this year's overall theme was "Parallel Dimensions," some of my fellow con-goers were already in a favorable mind for commentary. Between them and others online, the following observations and critiques of Sarah's writing voice, style, and substance came about:

> As someone who has Asperger's myself, I like this. Lacking social skills, an Aspie needs to create worlds to inhabit and characters to commune with. The world created here seems like an interesting place.
>
> – **John F. Mollard, co-author of** *MacGuffin*, **Virginia, MN**

> An interesting read, with lovely descriptives. I enjoyed the imagery it evokes, and I particularly love the touch of humour throughout.
>
> – **Druscilla Morgan, professional cover artist and co-author of** *Blood Of Nyx*, **Finley Australia**

Commendably ambitious. The rhyme patterns alone appear solid, conveying a lot of information economically.

– **Eric M. Heideman, editor of** *Tales of the Unanticipated*, **Minneapolis, MN**

Vaughan builds a vivid, engaging universe with a great depth of color and possibility, populated with fun and interesting characters.

– **Ozgur K. Sahin, author of** *The Wrath of the Brotherhood*, **Minneapolis, MN**

An interesting concept all round. Shows promise.

– **Jorge Salgado-Reyes Editor in Chief, Indi Authors Press, London, UK/ Santiago, Chile**

(She) has a distinct voice and a unique style of poetry that is daring and courageous, especially in scope and in application. She has a lot going on in this book.

– **Cynthia Booth, poet and co-playwright of** *Two Wives, and a Dead Guy*, **Bemidji, MN**

A poem-centric book with a big story to tell. A vast, unique universe is built and explored in brief, beautiful bursts of words in a variety of forms. Challenging to read, but a breeze to enjoy.

– **William Tucker, short story writer and novelist, Grand Rapids, MN**

And there we have it. Further proof that what you now have in your hands is not only an experimental tour de force but a rather decent read as well. And, if you really wish to support and help Sarah out further, be sure to leave a review on Amazon — even a simple "I like this book!" will be greatly appreciated by all involved, especially Sarah.

– **Roy C. Booth, author/poet/playwright, March 16, 2016, Bemidji, Minnesota**

Published by Whispering Petals Press
Copyright © 2017 by Sarah Teresa Vaughan

All rights reserved. No part of this book may be reprinted or reproduced in any way without prior written consent except in the case of brief quotations used in critical articles and reviews.
.
Published in the United States by Whispering Petals Press a division of Hawthorn Petal Press, LLC, Bemidji, Minnesota
www.whisperingpetalspress.com

Library of Congress Control Number: 2016934380
Vaughan, Sarah Teresa
50th Century's Prodigies A Noble Captain Bourn Episode 4 / Sarah Teresa Vaughan
Science fiction / Ancient / Classical composed with Elizabethan and modern English

ISBN 978-0-9847023-8-1 paperback
ISBN 978-0-9847023-9-8 E-Book

Printed in the United States of America.
Front cover illustration, "Threshold To Alika's Worlds"
Back cover illustration, "The Spectacle's Prized Crown"
All illustrations are property of author.
Cover design and interior design layout by TJ Studio, Bemidji, MN.

First Edition
10 9 8 7 6 5 4 3 2 1

*For William Shakespeare,
a bard I grew a closeness to, through his
plays, and poems. Endowed with great
influence, I recognize him as an inspiration
since my childhood.*

A special recognition for my loving mother. She taught me how to read, and chauffeured me to book stores, hence I can access any author, or enter any era, world, I desire.

Welcome to the 50th Century

It is the year 4991. Any time traveler touring this century will see alien beings from many dimensions dwelling together in peace. Alas, there art battles betwixt good and evil yet, to be fought. Events building prior to our tale, art: King Knock, whom is a creator in th' unknown heavens, fights King Aether, a black panther, having bat wings, along with his aid, Prince Agony, a giant praying mantis, whom has chronic Passive Aggressive Personality Syndrome, rebellious beings, whom art his enemies.

Lunar Morphosis, a wise sage, exiled from his home, Planet If, aids th' prodigies with advice, when dangers arrive. Dr. Amzi Hawk, a well-lettered scholar, dwells in th' Brain Chamber of Captain Alika's star ship, he willed his own brain to become the star ship's programming system, extending his life, whilst his conscience operates a grand vessel of the starry seas.

Multi-specie families art a routine normality to observe. Benjamin and Katar Geckerneck are an example. Not only are they different inter-dimensional species, their twelve adopted children are different inter-dimensional species.

The Mission Astro Regial Sector designed and launched the Region Paragon Leo Tolstoy EKK-4991-A. This star ship is a fortunate one, for her crew art the Geckernecks. The Geckerneck's main mission is achieving their search for Orbita.

The focus of *50th Century's Prodigies, A Noble Captain Bourn, Episode (4)* is, Captain Alika Geckerneck is aboard her star ship, reflecting on the first four years of her childhood. Within this episode is a construction of a vivid past bringing life to the main character. The first to have out, this episode is an overture to the 50th century as Alika perceives it. Reason being, is the main character's story is not only a grand entrance, but a dramatic history of her birth parents.

Attention! All tourists must remain in their time machines until they reach the 50th century!

Interior Illustrations

1. "Window To New Birth"
2. "Rhet & Sting, Ice Cream Men"
3. "Planet Tar's Ode"
4. "The Young Copernicus"
5. "Iwis, Forbearance"
6. "When Will Alika Hatch?"
7. "The Attack"
8. "The Curse Of The Fiddle"
9. "Escape From Planet Tar"
10. "And That's The Tale Of Our Nebula Cream"

Table of Contents

Fiftieth Century's Prodigies Theme Song
Dramatis Personae

Act 1: Th' Arts Of Galactic Youth
    Scene 1 Introductory Ode
    Planet Tar's Ode
    Scene 2 The Young Copernicus
    Scene 3 My Brother, V fán
    Scene 4 Down Town Planet Tar
    Scene 5 Envoy Of Scene 4 By Rhet & Sting

Act 2: Alika's Worlds
    Scene 1 Time To Hatch
    Scene 2 The Spectacle
    Scene 3 Actor's Childhood
    Scene 4 The Gaussian Invasion
    Scene 5 Planet Gauss

Act 3: A Battle Between Planets
    Scene 1 Gaussian Nature
    Scene 2 The Curse Of The Fiddle
    Scene 3 The Galaxies' Blessing
    Scene 4 Separated!
    Scene 5 The Aged Copernicus
    A Report On The Suffering Of The Inter-Dimensions

Act 4: A True Captain's Heart
    Scene 1 A Noble Captain Bourn
    Scene 2 The World I Traveled To
    Scene 3 Beings Of Steel
    Scene 4 Planet Tar's Essence
    Scene 5 Orbis Of Influence
    A Poem Th' Dirge Of A Space Alien

Bibliography
Glossary Index
Fiftieth Century Langue
Acknowledgements
Book Club Questions

50th Century's Prodigies

THEME SONG

Poem Form: French Ballad

Theme   The Mother of stars,
A nomad from M.A.R.S.
The Leo Tolstoy hath a crew
Who's lives art young and new.

Her captain, Alika,
Hath a woman's alma.
Yet, she is a prodigy
After a religious prophecy.

Chorus   A world prophesied, Orbita,
T' is where Alika
Desires to bring her crew.
Their hearts art young and new.

Alas, Orbita, is real!
How doth this captain feel?
There art those who wilt deceive.
Hard for them to believe.
Alas, Orbita is real!
How her crew must feel!
They hath th' eternal seal.

Encore   Th' Leo Tolstoy flies through many dimensions.
And is to creatures, th' main attraction.
As fast as th' speed of light,
Her journey is a passionate, passionate flight.

Composed by Sarah Teresa Vaughan

DRAMATIS PERSONAE

PLANET TAR, IWIS, FORBEARANCE

DR. CORNELIUS: A grandfather, historian, memoir, and poetry author, naturalist, and zoologist.

COPERNICUS: A father, herpetologist, limnologist, and author of memoirs on his expeditions.

ORKA: A botanist, composer of operas, herpetologist, mother, and musician of instruments; voice.

ACTOR: An apprentice, and servant of the family. He aspires to become a cosmologist, and zoologist. Presently, he is an alchemist, an author of science fiction, also, inventor of bio-artificial intelligence.

CAPTAIN V FAN: Their first bourn son. An alchemist, cosmologist, and a well known orator.

ALIKA: Their 2nd child, one of the future twelve prodigies.

Aboard the Region Paragon Leo Tolstoy Ekk-4991-A

RHETT & STING: Two of the future twelve prodigies. They are conjoined twins, each having multiple personality disorder. Chefs, poets, and singers, their constant personality changes correlate with their ever shifting gifts and talents.

Planet Gauss

CAPTAIN GLUTTON: A traveler of many two dimensional planets.

FIRST OFFICER WANT: Is not th' typical officer. He is a scholarly, obsessive reader, and writer. Always in want of well lettered company, he absorbs Manyway, and Jabez like a sponge.

COUNSELOR JABEZ: A language artist, and psychologist.

STAR-GAZER MANYWAY: A cosmologist, journalist for a Gaussian science magazine.

Act 1
TH' ARTS OF GALACTIC YOUTH

Rhet & Sting - Ice Cream Men

Act 1 Scene 1

INTRODUCTORY ODE

ENTER RHET & STING.
Poem Form: Ode

RHET & STING	We art known for our ice crème stand, making a secret, tasty cream. We even formed our own band!
	We art Rhet & Sting. Being conjoined twins, we art known as th' Two Headed Thing!
	Having a snake's body, we baffle visitors. We explain, "We art friends of ye."
RHET *STING REPEATS A 2ND TIME*	Hence, as thy friends, we wouldst like to tell thou, my friends,
RHET'S SOLO	of Captain Alika Geckerneck's birth. Do not forget her planet, Tar. Or, to eat our Nebula Crème first!
RHET & STING IN UNISON	Cause with eight arms, we mix it well.
RHET & STING	Alas, melted crème is an alarm!

Planet Tar's Ode

PLANET TAR'S ODE

CONTINUED BY RHET & STING

RHET   We wouldst like to tell of our Captain's
planet, her birth, her subjects.

STING   I'm gonna cry, I canst not stand it!
RHET   From the back or the front?
STING   Both eyes ye madcap!
RHET   Anyway, for the subject, thou get a hint.

RHET & STING   Tar's orb is still, never turning,
never a season, or a storm.
Mountains art never aging.
All their solar system's planets
art lined up, in a row.
Not a soul wilt believe it!

RHET *STING*   The moons Czar, and Star
REPEATS A 2ND TIME   Keep watch of the Gaussians
Over whom they wage war.
RHET'S SOLO   They soon, will encounter M.A.R.S.
STING   Not the ending! Doth not reveal it!
RHET   There yet, remain spiritual wars.
Alas, Tar's moon cluster
Wilt not let Gauss win!
O, to be Taranian!

RHET & STING   So, come to our ice cream stand.
We ha' the best to tastefully blend!
Succulent fruit, and skilled hands,
We ha' thousands from alien lands.
Our captain always comes to our stand.
Alas! We ha' a family that understands!

EXUNT RHET & STING

The Young Copernicus

Act 1 Scene 2

THE YOUNG COPERNICUS

ENTER COPERNICUS, ORKA, AND ACTOR.
Poem Form: Bestiary

COPERNICUS   There art many a galaxy to tour,
athwart the starry seas
for young explorers to journaly
take on space's desires, her aspirations,
whilst, lettered by strange beings.

I myself hast experienced canon,
within these years of green.
I, favoured by Planet Tar's ruler,
am given a palace of marble and precious stones.
At thirteen, I became a star soldier.

Heder: *Hebrew for royalty splendour*

His apprentice, I hadst the best scholarship.
Life in Heder 17, I taked on.

Alas, I met my dearest Orka!
Alas, I met my dearest Orka!
Taranian life is rewarding!
Baffled by strange customs, and faces,
th' venture into this city 't was spectacular.
Ways of life I ha' never seen or ever
in my life, on this planet.
Is there ore one way of living? Nay!
Some hath eight eyes,
others, three.
Some prefer to walk on th' floor,
others, th' ceiling!
Hence, I digress.

A fellow shed his skin,
 he could not see his way.
I taked his arm and led
this poor soul to his table.
From many a galaxy, he hast traveled.

I adapt to foreign tongues.
Folk gasp at my huge, purple eyes.
Large, cone formed sclera,
No iris, cornea, or pupil,
rich purple onyx t' is baffling!

So many things to do,
I muse of why I left.
Then again, I think I'm glad,
I hath a palace
and a new life to prep!

Poem Form: Norse Song Measure

ACTOR Ye told me this Sir,
 the day before, the night before!
 I ask thy requested questions.
 Ye tellest as though ye never told!

Ye art young Sir.
Having much to learn Sir,
I ha' never known
Such a story teller!

COPERNICUS My father wast a story teller,
Hence, I am a narrator.
I ha' many a tale
For being green of age.

ACTOR   Ye certainly do
Hath arrogance about you.
With a longevity of 2,000
We yet, ha' much to learn!

COPERNICUS   Yea, I grant myself credit,
Not even if I wanted,
T' is not mine to be shewn.
Alas, I admit it!

ACTOR   Ye art wise to do so.
Continuing on, ye go!
I still listen,
And ye doth go on.

ORKA COMES, HOLDING OUT HER FROG.

Poem Form: Blues Stanza

ORKA   Lo! My tree frog died!
He sings no more! He died!
His little lungs sighed.

Poem Form: Bestiary

COPERNICUS   I shalt get ye another frog!
It died young,
put him in a bag.
I shalt dispose of it.
Doth not ail thyself.

My father shalt be visiting us soon!
I wilt ask him to find a frog.
A zoologist,
he owns all creatures,
and is a student of them.

ORKA Splendid!
Ye and thine parents
art a chivalrous family!
Actor, do not keep th' frog in a bag.
Fetch a box; it shalt be buried.

ACTOR Aye my lady.

COPERNICUS I sawn a biped in th' likeness of a frog once.

ORKA Doth not tell me! In that city ye went to?

COPERNICUS How didst ye know?

ACTOR From the last hundredth time ye told us!

COPERNICUS Bless the mark.

ORKA Tell our neighbor about th' biped frog.

COPERNICUS Nay! Last time I knocked on their door
they yelled, "No more about th' biped frog!"
I shalt retire to my study.
There, I will learn things
of which art worth repeating.

ORKA Alas! Ye now knowst
th' art of conversation!
Study thoughts, ideas, and
events of others.
Then ye shalt be eventful.

Poem Form: Haiku

COPERNICUS   I shalt take my time.
Ancient works I will soon know.
My tea doth smell strong.
Planet Tar's moon gardens thrive.
Futurity, time,
Shape languages of children.

Tourists all round!
Alas, meekness t' is now, found!
My breed dost shew hope.

As need for sleep nears,
insects end their soft prating.
Crafts fly past gardens.

Argentine faces
gaze up at th' prim rose sky.
Reliefs tell the past.

Act 1 Scene 3

MY BROTHER, V FAN

ENTER COPERNICUS, ORKA, V FAN AND ACTOR.
Poem Form: Dialogue

	ENTER RHET & STING
RHET & STING	A replica of his father
	Prates on, even longer!
	He is e'en a star soldier,
	boasting of his adventures.
	He soon, becomes a captain.
	His crew always wins!
RHET	Alas, he is Planet Tar's hero!
	He yet, hast far to go.
STING	The next stage of Alika's history,
	will unfold, not tarry.
	What V fan is about to do…
RHET	Shalt baffle you!
STING	With an eye behind each of our faces…
RHET	We miss none of this tale's stages.
STING	Now, we prepared the Nebula Crème.
RHET	That fits the theme!
RHET & STING	A time before Alika, before us,
	t' was once much quieter without us!

EXUNT RHET & STING

Poem Form: English Roundelay

CAPTAIN V FAN	T' was a long voyage!
COPERNICUS	Yea! The age of pleasant, paradoxical voyages.

ORKA COMES FORTH

ORKA	V fan! Merry to see ye art well!
CAPTAIN V FAN	Mother! I also brought gifts for all!
ACTOR	I thought I heard someone call.
CAPTAIN V FAN	Doth ye fair well Actor?
ACTOR	Yea. Tell us more.
CAPTAIN V FAN	O! I shalt get into detail, farther!
COPERNICUS	Tell us Son! Thine eyes art larger.

Poem Form: Mad Song

COPERNICUS
Captain V fan, prithee,
Tellest thy great adventure.
Th' one when ye remained on board,
and thy crew went on break that day.

CAPTAIN V FAN
A giant of danger stood in my way.
A mass of grimly structure, it tarried.
Forth, came an abhorring voice of evil fury.

It lashed at my ship with its weapon.
Being a war prototype, it didst not move on.
Repelling it with a magnetic intrusion,
It turned away, in repulsion!

	My crew on Czar, mused on
	To find I returned from no leisure fun!
ACTOR	Why didst they leave thy ship in th' first place?
CAPTAIN V FAN	Only I wished to remain in space.
	This, they couldst not contemplate.
	They wished to explore Czar's tropical peace.
	I, tired of stopping from place to place,
	so, remained in my own space.
DR. CORNELIUS	I tellest, thus thou wilt see
	How their hatred came to be.
	Imagine a dimension,
	One that knowst isolation.
	Species befriend th' Gaussians,
	Yet, there remains confusion.
	Afeard, brooding.
	Either one chooses to live
	in strength
	Or, desperation.
	To deobstruct from regions,
	Planet Gauss changes their mission.
	Filled with rejection,
	E'en afeard of Taranians!
	Th' day Tar discovered
	A mystery t'was uncovered.
	Those in th' 8th dimension,
	Whom didst not like Gaussians,
	Ignored Taranians.
	In non-regardance,
	Of others' persuasions
	Tar continued exploration.

Poem Form: Sonnet

CAPTAIN V FAN   Yea, Grandfather!
                I remember.
                As a boy, I heard
                From teachers, true words.
                Th' history books lured
                One deep into Planet Gauss'
                   world.
                Rest assured,
                Tar doth not act afeard.
                We art not silenced by
                   Gauss' interpleading.
                There art few, good Gaussians.
                With them, we hope to ha'
                   reunion.
                To find them, wilt be
                   a great celebration!
                Lo, we must reveal
                   our true history to
                   all of them.

DR. CORNELIUS   Their wave thought, t' is
                a fierce weapon.
                Yet, we ha' peace as
                our destination.

Poem Form: Arabic Rubai

ACTOR   I saith, ye need a vacation.
Doth not age thy argentine skin!
Grant thy brain th' outdoors when ye can
Or, ye wilt grow into a stiff, rigid man.

ORKA   List to Actor, V fan.

ACTOR   Let us not be troubled now.
Let us ha' him stroll down town.
To take a spin, or walk,
woo't be a good thing to do, now.

COPERNICUS   Splendid!
Please it Orka, let us do these things suggested.

ORKA   Let him see all th' sights!
Actor, fetch our cellular hybrid.

ACTOR   Aye, Orka.

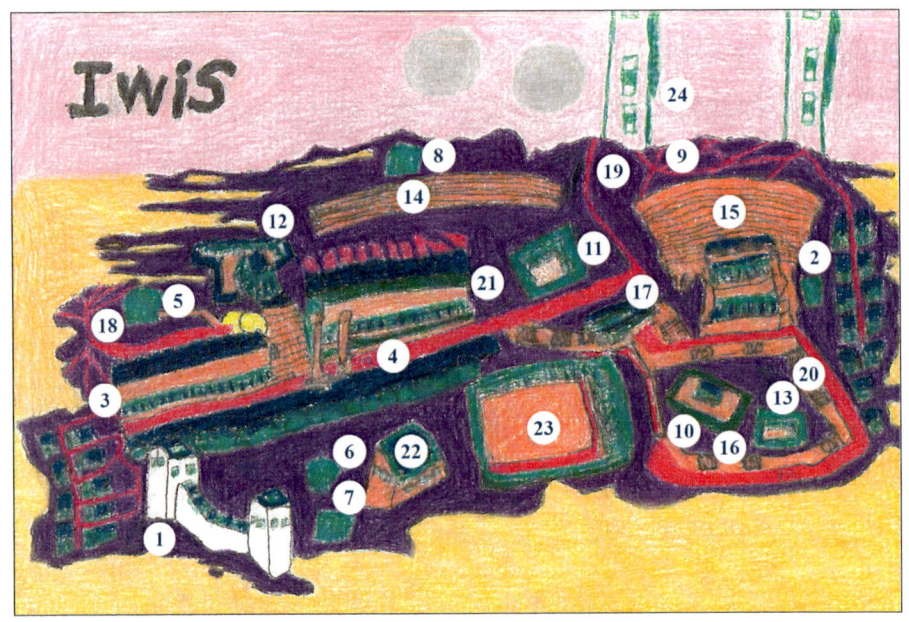

Iwis, Forbearance

KEY

1. City Defence Wall
2. Cosmic Gazer
3. On Acers
4. Lightway
5. Cosmic Gazer
6. Cosmic Gardens
7. Cosmic Park
8. Cosmic Court
9. Mount Violet
10. Olympeon
11. Steel Gymnasium
12. Giga Hall
13. Iron Gymnasium
14. Stadium
15. Red Coral Theater
16. Street of Mirrors
17. Galactic Council Hall
18. Street of Silver
19. Space Port
20. Metal Road & Metal Drive
21. Lapis Lazuli Chamber
22. Adamant Library
23. Commercial Growery Iwis
24. Space Elevators

Act 1 Scene 4

DOWN TOWN PLANET TAR

ENTER COPERNICUS, ORKA, CAPTAIN V FAN & ACTOR.
Poem Form: Pindaric Ode

ACTOR	No sound, a glib turn, a sleek craft
	With a conscience, and its own map, it flies.
	Telling it where to go, we LOVE our craft!
COPERNICUS	We wish to stop, and get some crèmes.
ACTOR	We will, once we show V fan the buildings.
COPERNICUS	Splendid! Show him the new apartments!
	They too, ha' space elevators for traveling.
ACTOR	Lo! See the screens of the virtual murals?
	They all read: THERE IS A NATURE SHOW.
ORKA	Why not show him the gardens which art floral?
COPERNICUS	That too! First the nature show at the park.
ORKA	Let us also walk the bridge!
COPERNICUS	Let us ask V fan what is his idea of vacationing.
CAPTAIN V FAN	I like the crèmes, the bridge, and the nature show.
COPERNICUS	Yea! Splendid!
ACTOR	Alas, we shalt go!
	Doing what we once did.
	Hence, we take on a serene trip.
	Now, that we got our crèmes,
	Pardon me, whilst I take a sip.
	Flying athwart this road,
	We art headed for the nature show
	Which is introduced in this epode.
	Meanwhile, we go on prating
	Of the latest news in Tar.
	Including a white hole we art investigating.
	It is time to get out, thus.
	We travel light speed, without a fus.

Poem Form: Keatsian Ode

CAPTAIN V FAN	Lo! They art serving food to eat!
ORKA	See? I told ye, to at least try it with us.
CAPTAIN V FAN	Let us try, and find the closest seat.

    ENTER DR.CORNELIUS.

DR.CORNELIUS   Welcome tourists! I brought
animals from all over Tar. First I would like
to shew an emerald exotic, th' Azure Wing Emerald
    Parrot.

Let's see how he sounds whence he speaks.

THE BIRD WHISTLES.

He is a hundred years old, which means his youth, yet
    Remains strong!

For ten years, the babies stay with their mother.

He is from our rain forests.
His strong beak is for opening hard fruit.

I wilt give him a treat.
Now, for the great task this bird canst do.
Bring out th' bioputer and shew us.
Splendid! This bird is able to do
math skills of a physicist!

THE AUDIENCE CHEERS.

DR.CORNELIUS   Th' breed learns complete sentences,
Curiosity t'is mischief perceived.
A lost mate th' breed wilt grieve,
For a month, its body, it will not leave.

Th' sharpness of his beak
is meant for cracking insect shells.
Th' purple streaks on his ebon beak,
art meant to attract the fish well.
Its emerald hue is so he canst hide
in the emerald flowers of our rain forests' trees.
His claws wrap all round my arm until
   he is ready to shew us how he flies!

THE AUDIENCE CHEERS.

Now, he will fly through hoops, from this side.

Poem Form: Ballad

Some planets ha' birds that migrate.
I'm glad that our birds never travel.
Seasons woo't be a dreadful fate.
In galaxies from afar, I saw strange creatures!

Some need skeletons to stand upright.
Just imagine being that type of creature!
I am glad we art invertebrates.
Th' spine canst cause problems, I ha' observed.

Poem Form: Sestina

ACTOR	Was not that bird amazing?
	Orka, did ye not think that outstanding?
ORKA	Yea Actor, I enjoyed it.
COPERNICUS	Let us see if my father is able to join us.
COPERNICUS	Father! How art ye?
DR. CORNELIUS	Of my adventures, I shalt tell thee!
	I ha' added to my zoo! I must shew ye.
ORKA	Alas! Ye hast greatly expanded!
	Pray, what is this winged quadruped?

Poem Form: Dramatic Verse

DR. CORNELIUS	T' is th' Spotted Dragon.
ORKA	Is this one a fire breathing?
DR. CORNELIUS	Nay, nay! Th' zoo wouldst be gone in seconds.
ACTOR	Th' turtles, I wish to see!
DR. CORNELIUS	We art headed that way.
	My wingless serpents art in th' trees.
COPERNICUS	Father, Orka's treasured frog died.
	To find one, I ha' tried.
DR. CORNELIUS	I wilt most merrily give any of my creatures to Orka.
ORKA	Father, gramercy! *(She hugs Dr. Cornelius.)*

ENVOY OF SCENE 4

BY RHET & STING
Poem Form: Sonnet Redoubled

RHET	Tonight, at our Nebula Crème Café,
	We ha' a special of great flavour.
STING	Withal sprinkles, soda, and berries.
RHET	All art a Nebula Crème lover!
STING	We also ha' an extra-large size
	With fizzing tastes of fruits sublime!
RHET	Trying this desert is wise,
	For, our new flavour is very fine.
RHET & STING	Too bad we ran out of fresh berries!
	Canst ye be our customer?
STING	Don't just linger, and tarry!
RHET	Will ye watch thy mixer?

Poem Form: Petrarchan Sonnet
with Italian Sestet

RHET & STING	On a trip to Pastoral Island,
	Escorted by Dr. Cornelius
	A noble captain is bourn, and
	She hath more wit than us.
RHET	T' was no event these parents planned!
RHET & STING	Alas! Her birth is a lesson, thus.
	Iwis, Forbearance will soon understand
	That they will soon, ha' a genius!

Poem Form: Sonnet Redoubled

RHET & STING	Customers art overflowing our tables,
Our shake mixer broke down!
We entertain with these tales
So that not a soul wilt frown.

Whilst Alika plays her Merry Nailor,
We scat along to her unique sound.
Now, we shalt return to our tale of her
And, find out when she comes around.

EXUNT RHET & STING

Act 1 Scene 5
THE WORLD OF DR. CORNELIUS

ENTER COPERNICUS, ORKA, ACTOR, CAPTAIN V FAN & DR. CORNELIUS.
Poem Form: Ballad

ACTOR	What do I think of Dr. Cornelius?
	He is brilliant!
	He is humourous!
	He is exuberant!
COPERNICUS	Actor!
ACTOR	A great scientist…
COPERNICUS	Actor!
ACTOR	He is fantastical!
COPERNICUS	Actor!
ACTOR	Yea, Copernicus?
COPERNICUS	End thy soliloquy, end thy song!
	Let us enjoy Dr. Cornelius,
	the fact that he lets us tag along,
	including all that he wilt shew us.
ACTOR	Alas! Th' azure-bellied water snake,
	th' prim rose-shelled turtles,
	th' giant, flame-hued, constrictor snake,
	and th' glistering, pearl-hued, river turtles!
COPERNICUS	Including seated in our craft for hours
	if ye must go on.
	Honestly, I truly wouldn't!
	Ye would, or continue to say on.
ACTOR	Ye ha' talent in thy humour!
	Although, ye are not sentimental,
	yet, thy father is also, a hugger.
	Watch him with his huge, feline animals!

DR. CORNELIUS	Alas! I ha' never met a soul whom knowst so much about me! Come! Ride in my craft. I shalt ha' my crew meet my family.

THEY DRIVE TO HIS ZOO.

Poem Form: Double Refrain Ballad

DR. CORNELIUS	My Lady, Orka, doth ye fare well?
ORKA	I am tired, and ha' been hibernating.
DR. CORNELIUS	Thine eyes ha' swelled! Ye ha' an egg that shalt be coming!
COPERNICUS	Father! This is mind boggling!
ORKA	I couldst not even tell.
COPERNICUS	For us, this is astounding!
DR. CORNELIUS	Nay, nay! I knowst clear, and well.
COPERNICUS	Ye definitely diagnose thorough. Orka, Dear, ye need to be resting! After the birth, th' egg will be put through an incubator for its period of growing. About its development, we will be learning.
ORKA	Ye certainly knowst well! I am surely feeling symptoms I remember well.
ACTOR	Whilst we aid each other through a time whence we should be rejoicing, We shouldst be thankful too. Miracles, too numerous to tell, will now, come into being. One thing ye doth know well, is that this canst be for uniting.

MISSIVE REPORT: A NEW CHILD HATCHES IN DR. CORNELIUS' ZOO

Poem Form: Narrative

Displayed in Dr. Cornelius' poultry incubator, which is placed in one of his display windows, sits a yet, un-hatched egg of a Taranian child. Tourists of Pastoral Island have this sight as the most desired spectacle to see. Many post cards, and gift shop items are featuring this sight.

This deep-blue egg, eight inches taller than his ivory, grey-spotted, bird eggs, is his new grandchild, and belongs to his son, Copernicus, and his wife, Orka, who live with royalty. They have a young, 100 year old son, Captain V fan.

The egg hatched while spectators pushed through each other to have a glance. Dr. Cornelius rushed in, and caught the child, peeling egg shell off her skin. They named her Alika. Her first words were an astoundingly, complete sentence. This child spake, "Thanks allot for throwing ME in with the birds!"

Act 2
ALIKA'S WORLDS

When will Alika hatch?

Act 2 Scene 1
TIME TO HATCH

ENTER DR. CORNELIUS, COPERNICUS, ORKA, CAPTAIN V FAN, ACTOR, AND TOURISTS.

Poem Form: Canzone

COPERNICUS
Father! Ye knowst we wert surprised!
I was completely unaware.
We never realized
There is a new being for which to care.
With many years of instructing ahead,
I have to, all over again, be a dad.
Taking in all of this, I dare.
Sith my aging won't make this easier.

Poem Form: Bestiary

DR. CORNELIUS
The mystery behind her being smart
Is that her brain is different.
Her corpus callosum, hath much calcium.
Her brain hath many folds.
It hath th' traits of an adult brain.

COPERNICUS
Her brain hath yet, many years of growth.
What will my child turn out to be?

DR. CORNELIUS
Sith the brain grows for such a long time,
and her intelligence is of an adult,
she is a child prodigy.

COPERNICUS   A child prodigy!
A new bourn that speaks as Ye, or I!
A challenge to all on Planet Tar?
She will become someone great.
I ha' just been committed to parenting!

ORKA   I am very grateful for Alika.
Th' universe needs more like her.
Perchance its music, or mathematics?
Why, she could one day, own this zoo!
Hence, I think she is a needed genius.

Act 2 Scene 2
THE SPECTACLE

ENTER DR. CORNELIUS, COPERNICUS, ORKA, CAPTAIN V FAN, ACTOR, ALSO RHET & STING.
Poem Form: Carol

RHET & STING   Brava! Brava!
Now, thou must have some Nebula.
We hope we see more of Alika.
Hey, nonna, nonno, hey nonna!

RHET   Was not Orka great?
She is opposite from her mate!
For praise, she is never late.

RHET & STING   *Hey, nonna, nonno, hey, nonna!*

STING   There is none like Dr. Cornelius!
He is th' animal's genius.
He always lives eccentric, and dangerous.

RHET & STING   *Hey, nonna, nonno, hey nonna!*

RHET   Now, about our Captain Alika.
She will challenge even Orka!
Poor V fan! We ha' a sad ending for ya.

RHET & STING   *Hey, nonna, nonno, hey nonna!*

EXUNT RHET & STING

Poem Form: Cobla

CAPTAIN V FAN	Now, having a new sister, I shalt shew her to my crew! Being baffled to see her, They wilt ha' little to say, and much to do.
COPERNICUS	Ye take care of her now.
CAPTAIN V FAN	I will, Father, I will.
COPERNICUS	Here art her things, and now I tellest ye, she never cries, is always still.
CAPTAIN V FAN	Splendid! I wish thou well!
ORKA	Behave, both of you!

EXIT CAPTAIN V FAN AND ALIKA

ENTER CAPTAIN V FAN'S CREW

CAPTAIN V FAN *(Addressing his crew)*	Audience! I would like to introduce One who is quite the enchantress For, she put our futures to great use. Lo! Here is Alika!

THE CREW CHEERS

She is my new sister.
Now, a year old, and a
Talkative one, we love her.

ALIKA	I am honoured to be aboard!

THEIR JAWS DROP.

Thou will not like my news for ye.
An enemy vessel is coming forward.
Our Captain knowst what to say.

CAPTAIN V FAN LOOKS TO SEE THAT IT IS SO.

CAPTAIN V FAN

Neuron blades up! Triumph over death!
Alas! A most dangerous vessel.
Gaussians! They nearly shot us dead!

(Looking at Alika) With Mom, and Dad, I am in T.R.O.U.B.L.E.!

EXIT STAR SHIP VELOCITY.

(Back at the palace, Copernicus, and Dr. Cornelius art having tea while Orka plays her harp.)

COPERNICUS Father! This headline is horrible!
DR. CORNELIUS What headline Son?

COPERNICUS My Captain V fan wast in near trouble.
(Sobbing) Both he, and Alika could ha' been gone.

DR. CORNELIUS Pray, let me read.

(Taking the paper) The Gaussians!
Heartless, from an evil seed,
Alas, art beings of two dimensions!

ORKA READS THE PAPER.

THE SPECTACLE
AN INFANT PRODIGY
OF SPACE

Poem Form: Narrative

There is a spectacle here, at the Purple Awards Center. Her name is Alika, and she is one year old. Yesternight, she saved the lives aboard the star ship, Velocity. This most popular ship is one of the main targets of Planet Gauss. She was visiting as a guest. It was a celebration for Alika. Having gifts for her, and cheering the fortunate 101 year old brother, neither he, nor the crew knew the fierce, Gaussian war vessel was going to kill them. After Alika baffles all with a mature greeting, mentioning the word "honour," she points out the two dimensional monstrous ship that would have destroyed all.

At the Purple Awards Center, Alika is the first infant in history to receive a crown, which wilt not fit until she is much older, for her service to Planet Tar, and Tar's moons. Asking Captain V fan how they might be greeted at home, he answers, "Alika will get all the attention, and I might be in BIG trouble with Mom, and Dad."

Iwis, Forbearance Missive Report

Poem Form: Common Measure

ORKA   Alika! V fan!
                    I nearly lost my children!

                    (Dr. Cornelius sets the paper down.)

DR. CORNELIUS   Alas, th' Gaussians
                    Mought be of 2 dimensions,
                    Yet their transmigration
                    T' is beyond our imagination.

                    In our region of space,
                    There was a clear break
                    In parallel worlds.
                    Quite baffling to daily take.

                    Worlds, interfering,
                    Art either uniting
                    Or destroying.
                    We need to be uniting
                    With those who choose to
                        be building.

COPERNICUS   *(Greets them.)*

                    V fan! Alika! Come to me!
                    We art shaken by
                        news of thee.

Poem Form: Light Verse

CAPTAIN V FAN   I must tellest thee
For th' sake of Velocity.
In instant humility,
T' were we.

ORKA   Pray, tell me.
How couldst Alika see?

CAPTAIN V FAN   On th' map for navigation,
T' is always an animation
Of a ship's location.
Behind me, is th' main screen.
Neither one, didst I see.
As for my crew's apologies,
They need new strategies.

DR. CORNELIUS, AND COPERNICUS GIVE HIM A STERN GAZE THINKING THUS:

V fan, ye did not see the ship?

ORKA   Poor V fan!
A brave captain,
We ha' thee once again.

(Actor completely ignores Captain V fan.)

CAPTAIN V FAN SLAMS HIS BEDROOM DOOR BEHIND HIM.

ORKA   I am talking with him.

ORKA KNOCKS ON HIS DOOR.

Poem Form: Ballad

                    V fan, in time, they wilt heal.
                    I see how ye feel.
                    Normally responding,
                    They art intensely musing.

CAPTAIN V FAN   Alika! She saved th' Velocity!
                    Most popular in th' starry seas,
                    This ship is raved upon
                          endlessly!

        ORKA   As an older brother,
                    Ye need to now, be a listener.
                    They wilt resolve in a while.

Act 2 Scene 3
ACTOR'S CHILDHOOD

ENTER DR. CORNELIUS, COPERNICUS, ORKA, CAPTAIN V FAN, ACTOR, AND ALIKA.
Poem Form: Chant Royal

ACTOR   My Lady, Orka,
Thy children art fortunate,
Both V fan, and Alika.
They ha' good parents.
A few hundred years agone, on this planet,
My parents looked after my childhood.
I had a father, whom I never understood,
And two mothers.
The first mother did all she could.
She was no child raiser.
I never had time with her!

Alas! Ye do love Alika.
My first mother worked, no entertainment.
So, spend time with her, dear Orka.
My mother hadst a social detriment.
She sewed, and cooked all food on this planet!
Thus, came an infection in her brain, from bacteria.
Lo! We became a phantasma.
For, she lost all memories, and knew not
Her husband, or her children, and it was drama.
I never had time with her!

My Lady, Orka.
Alas! I was now fortunate!
She changed, her first self was a phantasma.
Now, she became different.
She began to love her children, became a parent.
She spent all those times with ME, finding a
Way to connect, and be a better parent.
In a way, a blessing came sith the bacteria.
I now, had time with her!

Poem Form: Envoi of Chant Royal

Ye knowst thine Alika.
Mother knew me not.
Yet, she wanted to know ME, Orka.

I now, had time with her!

EXIT ACTOR

Act 2 Scene 4

THE GAUSSIAN INVASION

ENTER DR. CORNELIUS, COPERNICUS, ORKA, CAPTAIN V FAN, ALIKA, ACTOR, CAPTAIN GLUTTON, F.O. WANT, COUNSELOR JABEZ, AND STAR-GAZER MANYWAY.

Poem Form: Light Verse

Alika's family art playing a tile game. Orka entertains with her fiddle. A group of Gaussians art quietly looking in, and whispering.

CAPTAIN GLUTTON	Taranian music is just awful.
F.O. WANT	The song is writ backwards!
STAR-GAZER MANYWAY	Nay. This song is writ wonderful. Ore in this dimension, is it backwards.
COUNSELOR JABEZ	Th' song's mood is peaceful.
CAPTAIN GLUTTON	Backwards or forwards No difference at all! Destroying this planet is our call. It is fantastical Of how our people moved forward, How we got here, in tranquil, Through two different worlds.

The Attack

COUNSELOR JABEZ   Now, there is a void ye yet, hath to fill.

CAPTAIN GLUTTON   And I will fill it with working towards
Our target, Planet Tar,
For, destroying this planet is our call!
Officer, signal the ship forward.

F.O. WANT   Yea, Captain. I wilt not let our men stall.

EXIT F.O. WANT

STAR-GAZER MANYWAY   They are the very ones we should aim toward.

COUNSELOR JABEZ   Because destroying this planet is our call?

Act 2 Scene 5

PLANET GAUSS

ENTER DR. CORNELIUS, COPERNICUS, ORKA, CAPTAIN V FAN, ALIKA, ACTOR, CAPTAIN GLUTTON, F.O. WANT, STARGAZER MANYWAY, AND COUNSELOR JABEZ.

Poem Form: Blues Stanza

The Gaussian crew has sent more men. Alika and her family art placed into a wave thought due to neuro-blade torment, and art taken aboard their ship.

(Orka lifts her fiddle, which slid on the floor, after the neuro-blade exits.)

COPERNICUS *(Waking from his wave thought.)*	We must have taken a trip!
CAPTAIN V FAN *(Rises with Alika.)*	I swear! We must have taken a nap.
ORKA *(Playing with her fiddle bow.)*	Of course not! I wast playing! I took no nap.
ALIKA	They wilt torment their victims aboard. Wave thought erases th' victim's memory of course.
CAPTAIN V FAN	Alika! Thy knowledge makes my mind sore! Alika! Art ye not afeared?

ALIKA Of what should I be afeared?

CAPTAIN V FAN O, of the fact that we will be killed, Dear.

ALIKA We will not either be.

COPERNICUS How doth YE knowst, ye never see
The future, nor do ye ever agree with me.

ORKA Do not argue with thine own child!
(On her fiddle, she does a pizzicato.)

COPERNICUS O, me! We wilt be killed!
ALIKA We wilt not face death, against will.

COPERNICUS Alika is right!
She hath gifts, and one is *might*.
We must list to her, and cling tight.

CAPTAIN GLUTTON COMES FORTH.

CAPTAIN GLUTTON Greetings! I am Captain Glutton.
I shalt tellest thou thy lack of fortune.
Thou knowst not time. We shan't give thou one!

We wilt tear thy planet down.
Firstly, kill thy rulers, tear them down!
Second, we will killest thou, tear thy home down!

Last, we will tear thy planet down.
Not a soul will hear a sound
When we tear thy planet down.

ALIKA   It will be impossible.
                 There is a white hole,
                 It will shield Tar's orb all in total.

COPERNICUS   An eclipse!

CAPTAIN GLUTTON Children only list,
                 They do not speak, obey thus!

                 As for thou, unfortunate Father,
                 Ye now, must give them over.
                 For, thine home is taken over!

                 We will tear thy planet down.
                 Knowing *who* once hast torn us down,
                 We now, tear thy planet down!

                 EXIT CAPTAIN GLUTTON.

Act 3

A BATTLE BETWEEN PLANETS

Act 3 Scene 1

GAUSSIAN NATURE

ENTER DR. CORNELIUS, COPERNICUS, ORKA, ACTOR, CAPTAIN V FAN, ALIKA, CAPTAIN GLUTTON, F.O. WANT, STAR-GAZER MANYWAY, AND COUNSELOR JABEZ.

Poem Form: Bestiary

(Dr. Cornelius is soliloquizing how fearfully, wonderfully awe inspired he is by scientific observations of Planet Gauss.)

(Orka plays in largo on her fiddle.)
DR. CORNELIUS

Planet Gauss hath beauty.
Th' secrets of their solar system
art many.
Th' higher dimensional beings, canst travel
through walls, and alien elements
whilst on Planet Gauss.

Th' many worlds amongst us
keep revealing truth.
Tongues spake, reach athwart skies.
Imagine this world with closed eyes.

Gauss's streets art ivory hued, and polished
with a liquid appearance, sighted from space.
Many crafts, like lines drawn on paper,
move as ink, being applied.

Trees appear as drawings.

Whence birds fly, they art as lines.
As lead on paper, they appear
when they move, as two lines,
they raise their wings, becoming one line.
That is two dimensional nature.

Being 8th dimensional, our world,
all things art as under our feet.
Portals in Gauss' world, we see,
Within flat halls, as blueprints.
Their anatomy, as hieroglyphic art,
Forms with lines intertwining lines.
They couldst not swallow liquid from
   other worlds.
That is two dimensional nature.

Geometry, th' main structure,
Shews glibly through landscapes.
Steps appear as stripes.
Th' cube, Gaussians knowst not of,
Their scientists canst NOT decipher.
Nor art they able to create sculptures.
Lo, their atmosphere!

T' is in likeness of a drawn circle.

That is two dimensional nature.

ACTOR   King Knock of th' Universe
wilt take care of us.

COPERNICUS   We art doomed!

ALIKA — Th' Vagus Time Doorkeeper
           will open!
         They must move this ship
         or we will all travel to the past.
         Planet Tar's history would be dangerous
         for us to contend with.

COPERNICUS — Alas! Ye knowst history now?
             Things ye must not know, without school.
             Who taught ye this wisdom?

ALIKA — Grandfather did.
         Whence I was in an egg.

CAPTAIN GLUTTON — What is this whispering!?
                   Alika, tell me what ye saith.

ALIKA — Ye must move this ship
         or we will all travel to the past.
         Th' opening begins!

         TH' VAGUS TIME DOORKEEPER OPENS.
         TH' STAR SHIP IS VACUMED IN.

CAPTAIN GLUTTON — Ha! Ha! Ha!

ACTOR — Amazing!

(Captain Glutton gets eye level with Alika.)

CAPTAIN GLUTTON — Pray, Alika! Please it thy Grace, help us!

ALIKA — There is nothing I canst do.

CAPTAIN GLUTTON — Nooo!

The Curse of the Fiddle

Act 3 Scene 2

THE CURSE OF THE FIDDLE

ENTER CORNELIUS, COPERNICUS, ORKA, CAPTAIN V FAN, ALIKA, ACTOR, CAPTAIN GLUTTON, F.O. WANT, STAR-GAZER MANYWAY, AND COUNSELOR JABEZ.

Poem Form: Madsong

CAPTAIN GLUTTON, HIS CREW AND THEIR CAPTIVES, HAVE NOW, TRAVELED TO THE PAST.

LOCATION: PLANET TAR, 40TH CENTURY.

(Alika and her family art taken to the bridge. They must find a way to get along with Captain Glutton, to avoid death.)

CAPTAIN GLUTTON	Our lives art not over. Death to Planet Tar! We shalt yet conquer! We shalt destroy Czar, Star, and Tamar! Tar's moon cities, they wilt die sooner. Because of us, Gauss wilt grow faster.
ORKA	Sir, ye art ignorant. Thy ways, corrupted.
CAPTAIN GLUTTON	Thou wilt be surprised to see That we ha' a special place for thou. T' is Planet Absurdity.

	Take a while to absorb
	The fact that thou wilt be
	Sentenced to death, hearest thou?
ALIKA *(Whispers.)*	Mama! Play thy fiddle! Here, our music is backwards. It will make them ill. Swallow fear, and play thy fiddle!

(Orka lifts her fiddle and plays a prelude to a majestic dance. Captain Glutton and his crew crouch down, and cover their ears.)

Poem Form: Scottish Burns Stanza

CAPTAIN GLUTTON	Stop! Put down thy fiddle! What awful music ye fiddle! Thy sound is screeching, And thy bow is awful! Pray, quit playing!
CAPTAIN V FAN	It serves thou right! Thou thinkest thou ha' might. Lo! Over a fiddle, thou turn white! Thou love leisure, whilst we sit tight. Suffer through th' fiddle!

(Orka plays a danze macabre.)

Poem Form: Rime Royal

CAPTAIN GLUTTON   Long agone in Planet Gauss,
T' was an event between dimensions.
Planet Tar wast granted a pass.
It was a peaceful exploration.
Till one day, began a discussion.
A fellow conflicted with Gauss.
He knew not we woo't be aghast!
We hadst poured on us, Tar's arts, and math!
A world of illusions,
Hath thou never considered our vision?
T' would thou expect dimensions
To knowst each others' perceptions?
O, it ended in contempt!

CAPTAIN V FAN   Read our ancient scrolls.
Let not thy heart nor tongues grow fowl!
Tar's subjects hate not,
Lest she become of darkness.
(Orka ends her danze macabre.)

COUNSELOR JABEZ   Fascinating!
Both captains fighting.
Withal their might, defending
Their subjects' future.

Act 3 Scene 3

THE GALAXIES' BLESSING

ENTER DR. CORNELIUS, COPERNICUS, ORKA, CAPTAIN V FAN, ALIKA, AND ACTOR.

Poem Form: Narrative

(After a long while, th' starry sea oped her Vagus Time Doorkeeper, Alika's family takes over th' Gaussian star ship. Hence, Dr. Cornelius envisions a splendid model.)

A CROWD OF TOURISTS FILL THE PASTORAL ISLAND ZOO.

DR. CORNELIUS
(Holding Alika, he greets many who have traveled light years.)

Welcome beings from many dimensions! It is th' 100th celebration of th' Pastoral Island Zoo! I would like to introduce our new exhibit, an observatory formed of more than one glass chamber, its' lenses art adjusted for a view of 40th century space.

This glass chamber functions within my observatory exhibit, as animator, for us to view unique inter-dimensional regions of space. We canst select any review of history we wish. This day we choose that of my family's encounter with th' Vagus Time Doorkeeper.

We all remember what happed then!

My wonderful family, and I, prevented th' Gaussians from achieving their evil plans E'en though th' Gauss/Tar War occurred.

Let us now, enter! We must see how my granddaughter, Alika, is our little, champion.

Alas! We shalt enter th' glass chamber!

THEY ENTER.

We shalt insert th' 40th century lenses, which create th' illusion we left th' 50th century, and we shalt now, gaze into th' past.

Lo! We see th' space cities, and star ships of 40th century space. We art witnessing th' very battle! With th' press of my secret button, we wilt animate th' images.

TH' STAR SHIPS BEGIN ATTACK.

ALIKA Lo! Doth thou see Gauss's ships to th' left, and Tar's ships to th' right?

DR. CORNELIUS Alas! Wonderful, my Alika! Audience, doth it seem sensible now?

TOURISTS CHEER.

DR. CORNELIUS I shalt mark th' star ship my family and I were held captive in! Gramercy for attending!

THE SLOW, LONG LINE OF TOURISTS FILES OUT.

COPERNICUS   Wonderful Father! Ye ha' done it again.

DR. CORNELIUS   Done what again?

COPERNICUS   Create a popular showcase at thy zoo!

DR. CORNELIUS   Alas, without Alika, this would not ha' been exhibited!

                              EXIT DR. CORNELIUS, COPERNICUS, AND ALIKA.

Escape From Planet Tar

Act 3 Scene 4
SEPARATED!

ENTER DR. CORNELIUS, COPERNICUS, ORKA, CAPTAIN V FAN, ALIKA, AND ACTOR.

Poem Form: Ballad

(A wormhole storm has flooded th' atmosphere of Planet Tar. All Taranians must flee to their moon cities for shelter. A wormhole storm is a threat, for it can transport an entire planet to th' future anywhere in th' infinite, starry sea.)

(Orka is playing one of her many harps, Captain V fan and Copernicus art playing cards, to no surprise, Alika predicts, th' wins and losses. Dr. Cornelius storms through th' door.)

DR. CORNELIUS	Hark!
	A wormhole storm
	Hast flooded Tar!
	To escape this storm
	Wilt be hard.
	There is no knowing
	If we shalt die.
	We must start escaping!
	There is no time to sigh.
COPERNICUS	For our four year old child,
	We art done for, any minute!
	Our gifted child
	Wilt not survive it.
DR. CORNELIUS	This day, not real to me, earlier.
	Wormhole predicting,
	I knowst much sooner.
	T' is always frightening!

COPERNICUS   Let us hurry!
We ha' little time.

DR. CORNELIUS   People art in a scurry!
There is no time!

(Orka drops her harp. Captain V Fan, and Actor rush with her to Dr. Cornelius. They scammer from th' morning chamber, down th' hall of family lineage reliefs, out to the court yard. Th' wormhole storm is covering th' sky from a distance.)

Poem Form: Rispetto, Gaelic/Italian

ORKA   For my Alika,
There is something special I hath.
It will help ye with the
Way ye travel thy path.

ALIKA   A medallion!

(Orka takes off her ancient, gold, family treasure, and secures it round her neck.)

ORKA   This wilt remind ye
Of thy life with us.
We do this to protect thee.
We wilt miss ye, thus.

COPERNICUS   Ye knowst why
Ye must part with Tar.
Ye wilt journey
To another star.

	Alas! We, and Tar's ruler, Doth not wish for this. Yet, we, and our ruler Know what wilt come of this.
DR. CORNELIUS	Get thee in, little one. There is not much room, Dear Soul, We wish also to save our son. We canst ore save one soul.
	ALIKA GETS IN.
ACTOR	Ye art like a sister. I carried ye around. Ye art like a daughter, I taught ye our tongue's sounds.
CAPTAIN V FAN	Turn round Dear Ones! People art engirting around! Thy crowd is a silent one. The storm will take them, without a sound.
COPERNICUS	This is indescribable! Shut th' door on th' craft. It is unpredictable What planet will ha' this craft.
DR. CORNELIUS	Now, she wilt take flight! Our four year old child Is now, safe from this storm sight. Lo! The last we see of this child!

THE CROWD AND RULER GAZE UP
WHILE ALIKA FLYS INTO SPACE.

(The wormhole storm now, sucks Planet Tar into its vacuums.)

Act 3 Scene 5

THE AGED COPERNICUS

ALIKA AS THE NARRATOR.
Poem Form: Persian
(O, me! Planet Tar is no longer in her solar system, but she did amazingly survive her unwelcomed journey. Tar's subjects ha' become stronger, humbled, and more loyal. Planet Tar is in orbit within an alien solar system scientists cannot identify. Alika's family survived. Copernicus is grieving. He longs to see Alika again.)

ALIKA	His walk is brisk and his stance, arrogant.
	His cape glibly sways
	As he paces the palace of Elisábet
	Always facing th' heavens,
	He idolizes his past.
	Attempting to predict his futurity,
	He holds his head high.
	Hiding from his own grief,
	He sings psalms,
	Proving his beliefs.
COPERNICUS	Knowing not whence to sleep, to wake,
	I spend my time here, working.
	The ground seems to quake
	Whilst Fear keeps on breathing.
	For all subjects' sake,
	I have apprentices training.
	To others, of my art, they spake
	Spreading my name round.

COPERNICUS   No soul wilt forget
The day all of Tar worried.
The ruler, and all his subjects
Helplessly scurried.

To save Alika,
Tar sent her to safety.
All taken by the
Wormhole storm, quickly.

Took up all, with Planet Tar.
Lost in the future,
Souls ha' traveled far.
Alas! Tar saved my daughter!

Act 4

A TRUE CAPTAIN'S HEART

A REPORT ON THE SUFFERING OF THE INTER-DIMENSIONAL

Poem Form: Blues

Th' two dimensional pollution couldst kill them yet, here they standeth.
Subjects wear masks,

keeping gasses within th' Gaussian space crafts from killing them.
Streets, once bustling with merry
families art now desolate.

Th' nearest visible moons, Czar and Star, art sending aidance.
Th' blues is sad, yet we still live.

Feeling
is numb, the breeze peacefully blows, yet the rhythm is low.
A slow progress hast begun, citizens grieve
th, lost, yet the rhythm remains low.

Merchant tents hath fallen, and their owners taken! Scientists analyze the
grounds to ensure safety. A
plague of time travel braked out amongst us all.

Samaritans out from who knows where, art aiding those in need.
Our third farthest moon, Tamar, is
sending extra black hole powered sources to clean out clouds of these
wormholes.

A gifted master of rhetoric, Professor Peacefulness, is coming from
Planet Esperance to speak. We

knowst not much about this man, except that he hast mastered the
Gaussian tongue. His message is we

should come together and learn this language.

    Th' blues is sad, and th' streets art rough. Envoys are not needed because th' rhythm is low.

Faces
hath melted into marble stone. Th' rhythm is so low! Times ha' changed, yet none play th' part.

    Th' blues is sad, yet we still live. Feeling is numb, yet th' breeze peacefully blows, th' rhythm is low.

A slow progress hast begun, citizens art sad. Faces hath melted into marble stone.

Act 4 Scene 1

A NOBLE CAPTAIN BOURN

Poem Form: Fiction Narrative

A new uniform, with a gold medallion,
she is in likeness of a sage, her body is young.
All address her as Sir, Captain.
A green age
Perchance seven?
Folk gasp at her huge, purple eyes.
Large, cone formed sclera,
No iris, cornea, or pupil,
rich, purple onyx t' is baffling!
Th' year she left Planet Tar,
she became a star soldier.
Captain Alika's essence of Tar
Touches hearts all round.
Her brothers, sisters,
Each of a different species.
Lo! Fiftieth Century's Prodigies!
A crew of twelve, adopted,
By Benjamin, and Katar Geckerneck.
Their voyages, never ending.

Poem Form: Hymnody

A star ship, always sailing.
A strong family bonding,
For each ha' th' same destination.

Of Professor Peacefulness,
Th' young captain learns, thus.
To contact him, through letters,
She achieves!
After much searching.

Alika t' is yet, researching.
One day, she opes a history book,
Telling of th' days of old.
Within th' pages, t' is an epitaph:

A troubled star, without galaxy,
Lived through tragedy.
Chronic in illness, wounded,
Less than two hundred Taranians left,
Clung together and wept.

Act 4 Scene 2
THE WORLD I TRAVELED TO

ENTER ORKA.
Poem Form: Lullaby

ORKA
(Sings a lullaby on her harp for Alika.)

THEME	Buildings tower from afar
	Shapes sculpted out of stars,
	Shining through darkness of wars,
	Progress seems far.
	Let not thy heart go astray.
	Ne'er mind what worlds saith.
	Fireflies light th' path till day.
	A child sings, dreams time away.
CHORUS	Nursery rhymes, cradle songs,
	Elders learn from th' young.
	Starry seas, restful, wide,
	Hopeful that she survives.
CODA	In th' days of old,
	Our hearts were filled
	With thy tales told.
	Thy gifts began to unfold.
	Let not thy heart go astray.
	Ne'er mind what worlds saith.
	Th' dream ye love, live for it!
	Mayst in true joy ye keepeth.

Act 4 Scene 3

BEINGS OF STEEL

ENTER CORNELIOUS, COPERNICUS, ORKA, CAPTAIN V FAN, ACTOR, AND A MISSIVE OF THE NEWS.
(Missive of the news reporters art interviewing survivors.)
Poem Form: Sensory

MISSIVE Good morn!
I am standing at th' doorstep
Of th' palace of Dr.Cornelius.
Fantastical, ancient works of art
Amongst this marble, and stone
T' is a look into our planet's past.
Th' palace of Elisábet,
Land, a gift of friendship
from Tar's ruler,
to a unique family.
Scenes of feuds, romance, victory,
Famous kings, and their folklore,
Art proudly honoured within reliefs,
Ancient whispers behind awesome doors.
Scenes of triumph, tragedy,
Yet, all function as prophecies.
A history, teaching us
Who Planet Tar's Subjects art,
Beings of steel, for they knowst
Th' true prophecy of their breed.
Attention! Footsteps behind th' doors!

Poem Form: Dramatic Verse

COPERNICUS Greetings! Ye art welcome!
T' is an avalanche in my home!
Alas! My Alika!

My precious daughter.

MISSIVE Tell me about thy daughter.

COPERNICUS She t' was this home's joy.
We helped her flee!

MISSIVE Th' famous prodigy!
She is in an unknown century?

COPERNICUS We thought we woo't perish.
Her life wast my ore wish!

We knew ore one couldst flee.

Alas! Within another galaxy!

My wits left me!

MISSIVE Thy wits ha' not left thee.

COPERNICUS Doth ye ha' family?

MISSIVE Sith th' wormholes? Not many.

COPERNICUS We sent her in a tiny craft.

MISSIVE I pray she once again, joins thee.

COPERNICUS Woo't ye ha' done th' same?

And That's The Tale Of Our Nebula Cream

Act 4 Scene 4

A TRUE CAPTAIN'S HEART

ENTER RHET & STING AND ALIKA.
(Narration now, shifts from Rhet & Sting unseen by others, to uniting Alika with them. She is now, a prodigy captain living aboard her very own star ship, the Region Paragon Leo Tolstoy, EKK-4991-A with her adopted parents.)
Poem Form: Dramatic Verse

CAPTAIN ALIKA	Art thou chef personalities today?
RHET & STING	Yea! We art Rhet & Sting.
RHET	What was th' dinner ye ordered today?
CAPTAIN ALIKA	Scarlet Eggs.
STING	Hard boiled?
CAPTAIN ALIKA	Gramercy.
	I pray, grant me a Nebula Crème Smoothie?

Poem Form: 16th century song

RHET & STING	Coming up!
	Th' night t' is past,
	Another day, this vessel hath,
	Amongst th' tapestry of stars,
	We spend yet, another day.
	Singing a –down a –down a –down a!
	Th' horizon round this vessel
	T' is orient, deep-purple,
	Th' flowers art of a merry bloom
	Singing a –down a –down a –down a!
CAPTAIN ALIKA	Splendid!
	Far better than th' first song.
RHET	What art ye logging?
STING	I guessed it! A POEM FORM?

Poem Form: Carol

CAPTAIN ALIKA   Yea. I'm guessing thou wish to hear it?

                          Musing of my early years.
                          Laughter, love, tears.
                          Planet Tar, her subjects, star soldiers,
                          My birth father, and mother.

                          Alas,
                          Just reflecting.
                          My purpose t' is ore beginning.
                          Th' journey I am taking,
                          T' is ore forming.
                          I knowst not what I am becoming.

RHET & STING   Me neither! Me neither!

CAPTAIN ALIKA   Ha, ha! Very funny.
                          Shalt I continue?

RHET & STING   Prithee, read on!

CAPTAIN ALIKA   My Brothers, merry twins,
                          My heart, thou always win.

RHET & STING   Aaah.

CAPTAIN ALIKA   I now, digress.
                          Mayst I speak with my audience? Attention!

Poem Form: Tanka

Futurity
t' is full of strangeness isn't it?
In many ways, we canst be bourn.
How is it some art scholarly?

Names, why doth parents choose them?
This day, whenas a hole t' is filled,
Let thy growth of wisdom
nurture within.

RHET & STING   Brava! Brava!
Cheers for Alika!

CAPTAIN ALIKA   I pray, wilt thou come forth again?
Good night at once, to one and all!

EXIT CAPTAIN ALIKA

Poem Form: Satirical Epitaph

RHET   Captain Alika
loves poetry.
Her ne'er ending quill
gives her readers a thrill.

STING   Captain Alika
Hath a true captain's heart.
She ne'er is apart
From th' starry seas' heart.

EXUNT RHET & STING.

Act 4 Scene 5

ORBIS OF INFLUENCE

A letter Alika writes to Professor Peacefulness she reads to th' galaxies out her window.
Poem Form: Scottish Air

CAPTAIN ALIKA   A hero in my dreams,
Thee enchant whence I hear ye.
Thine eyes, in likeness of
   th' starry seas,
Their hue, sapphire, art glassy.
Thy will to live breathes hope
   into me.

Thy life, nearly taken,
Hast been reshaping.
For beings, ye art voicing,
That they might quit fearing.

Ye see possibilities
Amongst troubled stars.
For beings whom ha' thy
   same injury hard,
Thine speeches send aid
   from afar.

A star, in theater,
Ye fill all with wonder.
Battles for thy life,
   a wheeled chair,
Thee art strength.
Thy words fight as spears.

A few years or ever adoption,
I lived in an orphanage.
Surpassing my green age,
   in th' great schooling.
I, a vacuum, absorbing,
Nor ever forgetting!

Great honour, I own.
Th' ancients' praises, moans,
Art ne'er silenced, though,
It seems they art hidden.

A relief, cold, strong, hewn,
How Tar's subjects haunt!
Beings, and their lives shewn,
Faces hath melted into marble stone.

The End

Th' Dirge of a Space Alien

A sample from Sarah Teresa Vaughan's other works.
Poem Form: Dirge

O, Subject of Orb,
Approve my eyes
Hear my organ cry out
Allow me to assail your ears
List to my organ cry from th' heavens,
   to Neptune's Empire!
I am privy to what wilt become of
   thine world.
I have been through many harrows,
Grief, and sorrows.
The future is auspicious,
Yet, there wilt be pain for us.
So, list to me, an elder who t' is not yet
   bourn,
I, who am not of thy breed, and
   from heavens that art foreign.
So, hear my clepe.
List to me,
For I'll be a friend to ye.
Hear my dirge,
For shedding tears is my strongest urge.

So hear the clepe from my soul,
Which is blanketed withal dole.
My soul t' is so thickly blanketed,
   that neither th' glimpses of th'
moon at night,
Nor Phoebus' cart,
Canst cheer my heart.

My cheeks art stained with brine,
    and my eyes art galle'd, for I ha'
    been grieving like Niobe,
In that, I am th' ore one of my breed,
    and my planet hast become like th'
    LETHE!
Within, seems infinite, stumbling
    on hands, feet, and faces which
    art reflections of myself.
I insanely gnaw at th' corses as
    Scarcity's hooves trample on my
    burning stomach.
My heart, my heart, t' is weak from
    propelling my blood with lack
    of nourishment.
My extravagant and erring soul
    t' is ore a finite memory,
For no one wilt discover me.

There is hope for thine breed,
For Orb t' is still in its first part
    of life.
If thou walks on th' narrow streets
    of Heaven or ever t' is too late,
You wilt taste the sweet beverage
    of good fortune, and success.
And now, withal my last precious
    gasp of air,
And my last drop of blood,
I shalt write with true sincerity,

"God save you, Subject of Orb."

Bibliography
List of favored dictionaries & lexicons

American Dictionary Of The English Language Noah Webster 1828
Publisher: American Christian History Education
Copyright: *1828 Facsimile First Edition*

Anthology For Musical Analysis Second Edition
Author: Charles Burkhart Queens College
Publisher: Holt, Rinehart And Winston, INC.
Pgs: 563
Copyright 1964, 72

The Book Of Forms Third Edition
Author: Lewis Turco
Publisher: University Press Of New England
Hanover and London
Pgs: 301
Copyright 2000

The Columbia Dictionary Of Quotations From Shakespeare
Authors: Mary and Reginald Foakes
Publisher: Barnes & Noble
Pgs: 403
Copyright: 1998

Shakespeare's Words a Glossary & Language Companion
Authors: David Crystal & Ben Crystal
Publisher: Penguin Books
Pgs: 650
Copyright 2002

Shakespeare Lexicon And Quotation Dictionary
Volume 1 A-M Pgs: 755 Volume 2 N-Z Pgs: 755-1484
Author: Alexander Schmidt
Publisher: Dover Publications Inc.
Copyright: Both volumes unabridged as published in 1902; first published in 1971 by Dover

Glossary Index

Alma	Spanish I, for soul.
Argentine	Silver
Athwart	Across
Azure	Blue
Baffled	An expression of surprise. Eluded by shifts or terms of stratagem.
Beastiary	A poem form usually teaching about or celebrating any type of animal.
Braked	Elizabethan past tense of break.
Brooding	Sitting on; covering and warming; dwelling on with anxiety.
Canon	The Old Testament Torah considered to be prose. Also, it is a fugue in music.
Corpus Callosum	In the brain, a band formed of white matter connecting the cerebral hemispheres.
Damask	A pattern having two or more colours.
Dance, *Danse,* *Danze* **Macabre**	Morbid dance
Elisábet	Elisabeth
Engirt	Surround
Flame-hued	Yellow
Ivory-hued	White
Iwis	To surely, certainly know.
Largo	Slow
Lo	Look
Metallic	Elizabethan English for mechanical.

Missive	A reporter of the news, a messenger.
Onyx	A stone, either black, or deep purple in colour.
Ore	Only
Pastoral	A poem form that tells a tale in sequential lyrics, also a symphony of three or five variations. Beethoven's *Pastoral Symphony* is an example.
Pizzicato	To pluck the strings with your fingers, or a plucking imitation with the bow, keeping a steady, fast beat.
Pray	Used in place of please.
Prelude	An air, irregular, and short, played before the actual piece. There are some that seem to contradict this.
Primrose	The flower Primula, a pale pink.
Prithee say on	Please, do tell! Continue.
Retina	Formed of nerve tissue, this is the eye's inner layer.
Saith	Say
Sclera	The eye's outer layer formed of fibrous connective tissue.
Shew	Show
Spake	Elizabethan past tense for spoke.
Starry sea	My reference to the universe.
Vermilion	Red, or cedar.
V fan	From an Ethiopian to Arabic chart of scematics. The chart only shows the scematic in these languages.

50th Century Langue

*The * indicates that the author created the word.*

Alika*   A name inspired by the Hebrew name, Elika which means "my God has arisen" or, "my God has vomited." In Hebrew, there are many ways to use a word, and definition changes are numerous.

Bioputer*   It is similar to the computer, yet is a mind formed as a collective artificial intelligence co-existing with living beings.

M.A.R.S.   Mission Astro Regial Sector. In Alika's world, it is a famous nation in space populated by a society, sharing the purpose of exploration.

Merry Nailor   A fiftieth century, alien, piano.

Neuro-blade   A weapon similar to a laser, yet of unusual technique, and form.

Orbita   Classical Latin for orbit. In Alika's world, it is a place where beings from many dimensions spend eternity.

Starry seas   Outer Space

Vagus Time Doorkeeper   A name fiftieth century beings recognize the Einstein-Rosen bridge by.

Wave thought   A form of seizure the Gaussians can trigger with two dimensional neuro-science techniques.

Acknowledgements

I have attended numerous poetry classes and retreats through Headwaters School Of Music And Arts taught by Carol Ann Russell. She has been steadfast in encouragement, and supportive of my work. She wrote the preface for my first book, *Where Is Reality? An Aspie Poet Asks*, and taught a class on my science fiction series. She is my mentor, teacher, and close friend.

Wendell Affield, who is dear to me, is an author, and publisher who has graciously mentored me throughout the process of self-publishing my books. His friendship and advice, I highly treasure.

Lonna, who is dear to me, has been supportive, not only for each book I write, but also was there during chronic health struggles I have had. She is a wonderful aunt, who became a close friend, steadfast in encouragement.

Tracy is a true friend, who is always there for me, in steadfast kindness, and support. She encourages me in all that I do.

Book Club Questions

1. The "Prince Of Mathematicians" Carl Friedrich Gauss' work, through Michio Kaku's books, inspired Sarah to create the Gaussians. In what ways might she be able to empathize with these two dimensional beings?

2. Captain Alika Geckerneck's species, the Taranians, are eighth dimensional. Even though they have many advantages over the Gaussians, such as "their ability to see all of their organs, perform surgery without cutting into them, or cause death by offering water to drink" how is it the Gaussians are yet, able to have advantages over them?

3. The Gaussians hear music by any higher dimensional specie, as composed backwards. Discuss reasons how might this popular theory apply to a world in which, multiple dimensions co-exist.

4. Would you as a parent, send your child, regardless of their age, to an unknown galaxy, knowing by this, they will be saved from the dangers, or death, due to a planet's destruction?

5. How might Sarah's lenses allow for a two dimensional being to function in a three dimensional world?

6. Why did not the first bourn brother, Captain V fan, ever feel betrayed, or complain about her being chosen?

7. How might inter-dimensional travel alter culture, and sociology?

8. What is the moral message of our Taranian family's actions?